BURPING
BERTHA

Also available from Michael Rosen and Tony Ross:

Fluff the Farting Fish
Choosing Crumble
Don't Forget Tiggs!
Bilal's Brilliant Bee
Barking for Bagels

BURPING BERTHA

MICHAEL ROSEN

ILLUSTRATED BY **TONY ROSS**

Andersen Press

First published in 1993 by
Andersen Press Limited,
20 Vauxhall Bridge Road, London SW1V 2SA
www.andersenpress.co.uk

This edition published in 2014
Reprinted 2019

British Library Cataloguing in Publication Data available.

ISBN 978 1 84939 406 2

Printed and bound by Clays Ltd, Elcograf S.p.A.

It all started one morning in late December in a small flat in London, England. Nine-year-old Bertha was lying in bed looking at her old, trusty, cuddly toy, Tiger, when she burped, and Tiger fell over.

Downstairs she talked to dark-haired, blue-eyed 33-year-old Mum about it. 'Mum, I burped and Tiger fell over.'

2

'Poor old Tiger,' said Mum.

At school that day, Bertha had just finished her dinner when she burped and classmate Korvinder's cup fell over. Korvinder thought she had knocked it, but Bertha

knew, oh yes, Bertha knew it was
the burp that did it. 'What a mess,'
said the dinner lady.

'Sorry, Miss,' said Korvinder.

In the playground she moved
swiftly towards ten-year-old jeans-
wearing Shane.

'Shane, can you burp whenever
you want to?'

'Yep.'

'Can you teach me?'

'Sure,' said Shane. 'It's just gulp, swallow, wait and burp.'

After school that night, Bertha rushed to her room and put in

hours of burp practice. Gulp, swallow, wait . . . and nothing.

Gulp, swallow, wait . . . and nothing.

Gulp, swallow, wait . . . and BURP! and the sea-shell fell off the chest of drawers.

Gulp, swallow, wait and BURP! And the poster fell off the wall.

'Stop stamping around in there,' shouted Mum.

Life had changed for Bertha.

That weekend dark-haired, blue-eyed Mum and Bertha went to sixty-three-year-old Grandad's house. Bertha was soon despatched to the garden to collect up apples off the ground. She did for a bit, until she got bored.

She looked up into the tree. There's a juicy one, she thought.

Gulp, swallow, wait and BURP! The burp flew out of her mouth and hit the juicy apple. Down it fell to the ground.

BURP! and another . . . and another.

Grandad called out of the window, 'Don't just wait for them to fall, pick them up off the ground like I told you to.'

Bertha now knew she had a burp that was big; she had a burp that went just where she wanted it to and yet . . . people couldn't tell it was the burp doing the business.

That night sixty-three-year-old
Grandad took them to a show.
It was terrible. The clown wasn't
funny. The mono-cyclist kept
falling off. The singer screeched.

Then on came the red-haired,
green-eyed juggler. Oh, he thought
he was good. He thought he was
terrific. Until Bertha got going.

Gulp, swallow, wait and BURP!
Away went the red-haired,
green-eyed juggler's plates and
crashed to the floor.

'Say excuse me,'
said Mum.

Next week at school Bertha got bolder and bolder.

She hated the way the boys took up the whole playground with their game of football so she stood near

the goal and waited. Greg booted the ball straight at goal, Bertha let fly with a burp and the ball flew straight back at Greg. A few minutes later Stevie headed the

ball hard at goal – a burp from
Bertha and the ball was whizzing
back at Stevie's head. A few more
of these, and the boys got fed up,
started arguing with each other
and went off to play Terminator
games. The girls had that part of
the playground to themselves and
played American football there.

At Bertha's school nobody liked balding forty-two-year-old Mr Fobnitch. He shouted too much and if he was really angry he grabbed children's arms and squeezed them so hard it felt like their hands would drop off. Bertha saw him

grab her friend Shakira and yell
right in her face. Bertha let fly the
burp and next thing his glasses
were flying through the air.

Maybe balding forty-two-year-old
Mr Fobnitch was horrible but he

was also cunning. He didn't know how his glasses flew off but he was sure it was something to do with Bertha. He took to spying on her with his binoculars out of the staffroom window at playtime. He started to notice how wherever Bertha went in the

playground, something strange
started happening. Footballs seemed
to wiggle in the air, skipping ropes
seemed to get knotted up and

hats never seemed to stay on
people's heads. And what was
that happening now?

Balding forty-two-year-old Mr Fobnitch watched through the binoculars and there was Bertha with a grin on her face. Now he got out his special triple power navy telescope and fixed it on

Bertha's face. She was moving
across to Brad – big, tough Brad
was just shoving Georgiou halfway

across the playground when all
of a sudden he was staggering
backwards even faster. But Mr
Fobnitch has seen something else.

He saw Bertha's gulp, the swallow,
the wait and then the burp.

'That's it,' he shouted and he was
down on to the
playground.

Bertha was taken in to see fifty-two-year-old, lightly tinted-haired Mrs Bouncible.

'I think I have made a discovery,' said Mr Fobnitch. 'This young lady is wreaking havoc, causing disaster wherever she goes. I'm not sure exactly how she's doing it, but it's something she's doing with her mouth.'

'Bertha dear,' said Mrs Bouncible, 'this doesn't sound like you. Is there anything in what Mr Fobnitch is saying?'

Bertha went quiet. What could she say?

'Ah hah,' said Mr Fobnitch, 'the silence of the guilty.'

'Well, Bertha?' said Mrs Bouncible.

Bertha waited for a moment and then told all. Out it all came, the morning with Tiger, learning from Shane, the apples, the juggling . . .

'. . . and my glasses,' said Mr Fobnitch.

'Well, well, well,' said Mrs Bouncible. 'You know something, Bertha? Maybe you could do it for our Christmas Concert.'

So that's how it was, that at Charlie Chaplin Primary School's Christmas Concert that year, after 'Away in a Manger' and before 'Rock Around the Clock', Bertha stood up in front of all the parents and children and she knocked

chocolate Santas off the Christmas
tree from the other side of the hall
with some of the biggest burps.
Everyone loved it.

Now it so happens that one of the parents at the school, Josephine's mum, who was also called Josephine, worked for the local newspaper. So just for a bit of fun at Christmas she put in a story that went like this:

BERTHA THE BURPER

Parents, teachers and children at Charlie Chaplin School were soon rocking in their seats at their Christmas Concert last week when young Bertha Cuckoonest performed her piece. But she wasn't just blowing their minds – chocolate Santas were taking a ride faster and further than Rudolph could ever take them. Unbelievable Bertha was burping them through the air.

It seems like this young explosives expert can launch a burp that . . .

Next day the story appeared in the national newspapers too:

THE TIMES

Miss Cuckoonest's Christmas Surprise

The National Curriculum makes no mention of events such as the one that took place at a school concert earlier this week.

DAILY MIRROR

Exclusive

BURPING BERTHA BAMBOOZLES BOFFIN

Mirror science correspondent Professor Gordon Wunderkind said today: 'Wow! this is just one helluvan amazing kid.'

New Scientist

Genetical considerations apart, the environmental significance of a high velocity eructation . . .

The phone was soon ringing at Bertha's house.

'Hi, are you Bertha's mum? Great. I'm from a record company called Skunk Productions and my name is Freddie Skunk and everything I've heard about your wonderful daughter sounds – er – wonderful. Terrific. Look we would be very interested in making a record with Bertha. It would be a kind of rock-rap-rootsy kind of thing and Bertha would give it a bit of bass punch, you get?'

'Hello, is that Mrs Cuckoonest? This is the BBC News here, Bill

Eton speaking. We would very much like to feature young Bertha on the Ten o'Clock News tonight. Is that a possibility? Hmm?"

So that night on the News:

'And finally: yes, miracles happen at Christmas, young Bertha Cuckoonest has certainly stirred things up, not to say "brought things up" since her starring role in her school Christmas Concert . . .

'And so, Bertha, let's see what you can do with this coconut.'

And in a recording studio in North London:

Don't do that thing you know I hate.
Don't come here when you know you're
   late.
Just give me your love like you used to do.
Let me hear you tell me you love me true.

Burp-burp-burp-burp-burp-burp.

And that was another four microphones shattered.

In a laboratory in Milton Keynes, Dr Gladys Sulphate and her team of Eructologists (that means Burpologists) examined Bertha.

44

'Are we talking epiglottal over-development or pulmonary elasticity?'

'Burp!' said Bertha and the clip-board went flying.

The next letter to arrive at Bertha's house certainly gave them plenty to think about.

Dear Bertha,

We've heard the record, we've
seen the newsclips, we like it,
we like it a lot. We'd like it
too if you came to Hollywood and
talked with us about a script
we're developing at the moment.
It will star Madonna, Arnold
Schwarzenegger, Harrison Ford and
the Queen. It's the story of a
pop star who makes a robot. The
robot takes up deep-sea diving
and marries the Queen. Oh yeah? I
hear you saying, where do I come
in? Hold the phone, baby, you are
the robot's dog. Whaddyasay?

See ya in L.A.

Rip Sox

The film was called 'Snow White and the Seven Terminators' and had changed a little since Rip Sox's first ideas.

The Queen was now playing the part of Robin Hood and Bertha was

an alien. Arnold Schwarzenegger was now the dog. Bertha was re-named Dorothy, Harrison Ford was the Wizard of Oz and Madonna was the Tin Woman.

Bertha sang 'Over the Rainburp' but, it has to be said, she was never quite sure why the film was called 'Snow White and the Seven Terminators'. But the poster was great and millions flocked to see the film and buy it when it came out on video.

So of course, Bertha became a multi-multi-mega-billionaire superstar. Bertha T-shirts, posters, statuettes, board games, video

games, comic strips and cartoon programmes sold all over the world.

But like a lot of great stars, fame and glory led to disaster. One night, halfway between Nashville, Tennessee (where she had been recording 'It's one last burp on the long, long road to heaven') and Hackney, East London (where she was going to demolish fourteen tower blocks) her plane crashed.

Experts who examined the wreckage came to the conclusion that some kind of explosion tore a hole in the side of the jet close to where Bertha used to sit. It was noticed that the on-flight refreshments that night were: Jackson's Wizzofizzo Superplus . . .

But Bertha's name lives on.

Her home has been turned into a shrine called Burpland and more people have visited it this year than watched the Cup Final. Old tapes have been found of Bertha singing 'Twinkle, twinkle little burp' which have been given a re-mix with some of her best burps. There is a Bertha fan club with a magazine called *Safety Belch* and from all over the world reports are coming in that Bertha has been seen.

Who knows? Perhaps the plane crash was just a Bertha trick, say the fans, and really she baled out of the plane with a parachute over

Ireland and she is really alive and well and burping in secret somewhere . . .

Don't Forget Tiggs!

BY MICHAEL ROSEN
ILLUSTRATED BY TONY ROSS

Mr and Mrs Hurry are always rushing about. They never stop! But that means they sometimes forget some rather important things – like eating ... and shopping ... and taking their son Harry to school!

Thankfully, Tiggs the cat is around to remind them. But will anyone remember to give Tiggs his dinner?

'Funny family adventure. Brilliant for emerging readers'
The Bookseller

9781783442690   £5.99

FLUFF THE FARTING FISH

By MICHAEL ROSEN
Illustrated by TONY ROSS

Elvie is desperate for a puppy that she can train up to do amazing tricks. But it's not a puppy Mum returns from the pet shop with, it's a fish. But Elvie doesn't give up. Determined to fulfill her dream of having a performing pet she trains up Fluff the fish. Fluff can't sit, she won't bark on command, but she does have a very special fishy talent all of her own …

'A real treat for young readers, full of cheeky humour' *The Bookseller*

9781849395274   £5.99

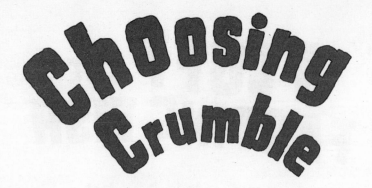

Choosing Crumble

BY MICHAEL ROSEN
ILLUSTRATED BY TONY ROSS

When Terri-Lee goes to the pet-shop she thinks she'll
be choosing a dog – she doesn't expect the dog to be
choosing her! But Crumble is no ordinary pet and he's got
a few questions to ask:

How many walks will you take me on?
Do you like to dance?
Will you tickle me? I like that a lot.

Will Terri-Lee's dance moves and
answers be enough to convince
Crumble that she could
be his owner?

9781849395281 £5.99